Samuel J Jones is happily married to Lauren. His three daughters, Isla, Jorgie, Luna, and their soon to arrive son are his world. The author has spent his adult life working in a job he didn't love until 2017 when he left and started his own company. This inspired him to pick up a pen and set out on his dream to write. He has written songs, poems and short stories from the age of eight, but at the age of 38, he is beginning to live out his dream.

To my wife, Lauren. Thank you for your support in my journey that led to this moment.

Samuel J Jones

THE ARRANGEMENT

AUSTIN MACAULEY PUBLISHERS™
LONDON • CAMBRIDGE • NEW YORK • SHARJAH

Copyright © Samuel J Jones 2024

The right of Samuel J Jones to be identified as author of this work has been asserted by the author in accordance with sections 77 and 78 of the Copyright, Designs and Patents Act 1988.

All rights reserved. No part of this publication may be reproduced, stored in a retrieval system, or transmitted in any form or by any means, electronic, mechanical, photocopying, recording, or otherwise, without the prior permission of the publishers.

Any person who commits any unauthorized act in relation to this publication may be liable to criminal prosecution and civil claims for damages.

This is a work of fiction. Names, characters, businesses, places, events, locales and incidents are either the products of the author's imagination or used in a fictitious manner. Any resemblance to actual persons, living or dead, or actual events is purely coincidental.

A CIP catalogue record for this title is available from the British Library.

ISBN 9781528937542 (Paperback)
ISBN 9781528969154 (ePub e-book)

www.austinmacauley.com

First Published 2024
Austin Macauley Publishers Ltd®
1 Canada Square
Canary Wharf
London
E14 5AA

Chapter 1

It was Steven's 16th birthday. As he looked at the unscarred white brick walls of his parents' 1970s house, he held the card he'd received that day in his hands. The old man who handed it to him had a tired face like he had met with a sadness no person should have to know.

He wore a faded green jacket with rips in, and a woolly orange jumper with a shirt and tie underneath. Before he left, Steven felt a strange sense of knowing and kinship with him which he failed to vocalise.

He observed a reluctant handshake between the old man and his dad, followed by an uncertain wave of the left hand from his mother. With the right hand, perched into the crease of her joints, her folded arms remained her primary body language as she obliged the handshake.

"Who was that man?" asked Steven.

"A distant relative," remarked his father, giving him a sense that he should ask no more questions on the matter.

Steven took the crinkled five-pound note from inside the card and added it to his pile, before revising some more in his room.

Doodling and scribbling, a few hours had passed when Steven looked outside the window and across the street was the distant relative, who came by earlier. He waved up at the window. Steven paused for a second, then involuntarily raised one finger as he mimed, "Wait there."

Closing the front door gently, he walked over to the old man and without hesitation, he asked, "Who are you?"

"I'm your granddad, boy," he replied.

Handing Steven a note, he explained that he was not welcome but had a duty to make sure this letter was received.

"Take care Steven. You look just like her," he said, as his thumb and his index finger met with Steven's chin. Steven watched as the man walked away. He knew there were questions residing within him, but understood, almost intuitively why the man had to leave, and so respected his departure.

Heading down the suburban cul-de-sac onto the next street and around the block, he buried his head into this letter:

I love you, Stevie, now most letters close on this, but there is not much of a beginning, middle or even an end to this relationship. I have a few brief moments to hold on to, and a picture of you that has come with me but you don't know me. You will probably search for the details as I'm sure you always have, but you will not find much. I cannot offer you answers, nor can I fill you in on any gaps. All I can give you is my life. My entire estate now belongs to you and it is yours alone and it comes with only one obligation. You embrace it. If you are lucky enough, you will get to live 80 birthdays and 80 Christmases. So, do live because it doesn't take long to count to 80. I will love you forever.

Yours Sincerely,
T

Steven folded the letter into perfect symmetry, creating a rectangle the size of a keyring. He placed it into his back pocket and made his way home.

"Steven! Steven!" he heard a voice getting louder…

"STEVEN!" hissed his father, ushering him to take to the podium.

Steven's long daydream of four years left him feeling empty and unanswered and moments before he was about to address a church full of people mourning his mother. With the idea that his real mother had a story out there and all he knew was that her name had the letter 'T' in it and some estranged old man was her father. He froze in that moment.

It was four years since he received his letter on his birthday and he never checked into the authenticity.

He knew he was adopted shortly after birth and that he was born in June in 1979, but there was little information other than that.

Steven's adoptive mother always wanted children and could not have any of her own. His father never seemed set on the idea of adoption and was a strict traditional man, but his love for his wife meant he supported her need to be a mother.

They were in their late 50s when they adopted Steven and they always struggled as he got older, to parent him in the same way his friends were raised. They were financially stable, well respected and cared for Steven but there was always a hole in the road when it came to building the perfect bond.

Their struggle to show affection was evident in Steven's upbringing. He was sociable, yet shy, athletic yet reserved. All the other kids would want to play out with him and all the young girls would ask him to the disco but Steven would rather read or build model cars.

Walking to the podium, Steven looked around the room to see ladies crying into their handkerchiefs, his dad's friends using the order of service as a way of cooling off the heat that was soaring through the multi-coloured glass on the high framed windows.

Licking his lips and brushing his bottom lip with the bottom row of his teeth, he prepared to start his awkwardly rehearsed speech and as he looked to his father, he noticed how his head was down and not even present in the moment.

"I love you, Mum! May you rest in peace."

He had more words prepared but he knew that his father wanted this moment to be over and so Steven wanted to speed the process up.

"Thank you all for coming." He walked back to his bench.

After the service, he asked his father if he would like him to stay with him at the family home, but his dad declined. Steven knew that without his mother, to glue them together that this was not only the day he buried his mother, but it was also the day that he and his father began the ending of a very strange relationship.

Without malice or emotion, they simply co-existed until even the obligatory Christmas and birthday visits disappeared and they became merely strangers, who would nod in the street if they happened to bump into one another. The strangest notion of all this was that they both had a mutual level of respect for each other's honesty.

Steven would go on to live the next two years in his rented two-bedroom apartment, outside of Manchester. Over the years, he would go on a few dates but had little interest in messing around.

Steven was considered to be boyishly good looking, yet he never really knew it himself. He was 5ft 11in with a very short, trimmed beard. He had blue eyes and chiselled cheekbones. He wore a diamond stud earring in each ear, and he would always wear a cap with a peak that hid the top end of his head and he had quite feminine eyelashes with perfectly straight teeth. He had a bounce in his step and when he walked his little finger on his right hand would always point slightly outwards. This used to make him paranoid when he was younger, so he would often clench his fist in a ball, which would subsequently make him look slightly aggressive. He was calm, quiet and well mannered. In his younger years, he was always invited to join in social events with other kids, but he often declined, yet he was never considered strange or an outcast. He was seen as a cool character that would not conform to any type of clique. He was more of a shepherd than a sheep but didn't want or desire any followers.

He worked as an assistant manager for a high-end wine bar on the outskirts of town and kept himself to himself. That's until he met Stephanie.

Chapter 2

It was October 2001 and Steven continued a two-year episode of flirting with Stephanie, the young girl who worked the weekend shifts.

Steven could not intentionally flirt, in his case, it was more of an act of consciously making any attempt possible to use any way of contact to respectfully express his inhibitions.

In his eyes, she was the special one. She had stunning long brown hair, dimples on her cheeks, eyelashes that looked like they had been painted on to perfection with a feather pen, her voice was delicate and timid and she smelt like spring, no matter how long she had been working. She was small and petite and had a tattoo down the side of her thumb that said 'princess' which is what she called her daughter. She had beautiful white teeth and freckles on the right side of her face. Her left eye was slightly lazy, but she never wanted to wear her glasses, so she would sometimes talk and look as though she was seeing through a smoky mist, but this added to the attraction for Steven.

He fell in love with Stephanie the moment he saw her two years back and unlike any other instances in his life, he was not afraid to tell her.

They would phone each other late at night. They would go out on walks together and accidentally on purpose, always plan to bump into each other when they were on a night out.

It was as though they were made for each other. There were clear signs that she thought very highly of Steven too but she would never take him up on his offer to go out romantically.

He would joke that they were 'The Two Stes' and that became their secret team name they gave themselves.

Stephanie had a young girl to a guy, who was extremely possessive before she separated from him. He was her high school sweetheart, who for no known reason, started to emotionally abuse her once their baby was born. Like a jealous reaction.

Steven would even use this issue to get close to her. He would tell her that he had looked into cases for her and foolishly explain researched facts that he read like how one in six abused women report that their partner first abused them during pregnancy, and at least 4–8 per cent of pregnant women report suffering abuse during pregnancy.

He must have thought that this would bring him closer to her and that the information would prevent her from ever falling back into a relationship with this man.

This was hard to take for Stephanie, because in the years, before their baby girl, her partner had never treated her in any way but with kindness so it confused her that the man she fell in love with, would do this and so she had to leave him when she did.

Steven resented her when she would bring him up in conversation in a positive manner. If she ever talked of him in a positive way, he would jump in with a sly comment like, "If an abuser strikes his partner once, he's likely to do so again," and then they would fall out and sulk with each other and give each other the silent treatment for several days until Steven would contact her with a silly message saying, "Are we still friends," and moments later, 'The Two Stes' were back as a team.

Steven struggled to understand why their connection, their perfect little serendipitous coincidences and all the tiny and strange things they had in common, would not be enough to help her fall for him.

He even made it clear that he would be there as help to raise her daughter. He would buy her gifts at Christmas and Stephanie was too polite to tell him that he was stepping over the line but nothing he could say or do would convince her to be with him, she would simply remind him how amazing he was and assured him that he would meet 'the one,' one day and that he was too good for her.

Steven was very cool and controlled in most circumstances but when it came to Stephanie, he was far too intense. He was very full-on and like a drug or a spell, he could see when he was behaving foolishly but could not refrain himself from doing so.

He would sometimes attempt at leaving her alone for long periods of time but then Stephanie would miss his company and, in some ways, miss the idea of a good person who sees her in a way that other men won't look to see.

She would get back in touch with him and then the spell would start again, and because she would be the one getting in touch, he would misinterpret this as she was finally falling for him.

Steven just could not let anybody else in when it came to love and many tried, but for him, it was Stephanie or nobody.

It was October and it was Halloween night in the bar. Steven was excited because it was a big fancy dress ball theme and he still hoped to get the girl of his dreams.

He was walking into his shift feeling very confident. Dressed as a very stylish vampire, he had mixed the perfect combination of festive-themed and slick classy attire. He believed that this night was his night because their flirting had intensified to a level he had not known before. The last few times they spoke, she insisted that he made the effort to go into town after it and she implied that they would share a taxi home and that she may even 'crash on his couch'.

Walking through the back of the kitchen to go to the staff break area, he recognised her perfume and smiled so much so that the skin on his cheek reached the bottom of his eyelids, he could not wait to see her.

He wanted to sneak in the room as it's only fitting that he scared them on Halloween night and as he peered through the door his heart fell to his pelvis.

Stephanie was kissing one of the bar staff. Greg, the actor. The guy who everyone knows is a ten. She looked so happy in his arms. Though it could just be a drunken kiss, Steven took offence at every single previous situation where she had said she did not want to be with anybody at all. All of a sudden, every intimate conversation became, in his eyes, moments where she had been leading him on and laughing at him behind his back.

In one split second, his heart had broken and he hated himself because he knew he would still be the first to call her in time and he would still have a spot in his heart where he believed he was the one to make her happy and that he could still win her over.

Steven left the building and called for a taxi and as he was wiping off the black lipstick from the lids of his eyes as he was replaying the worst moments he had ever seen.

Pulling up to his apartment, he handed 20 pounds to the driver and walked to his building gate, as a group of drunken students cheered and chanted past him, he stood back to a clear space on the curb, as he put his right leg back he lost balance but was quick enough to recover, he swiftly moved forward and walked into a stranger. "It's you?" Steven asked.

"You are the old man from my birthday? You said you were my granddad?"

"You never signed the deeds or followed up anything from the letter," the old man said, who looked even more tired whilst holding his breath with a whistling hiss in each word.

Steven wanted to take out his newfound heartbreak on the old man, but it was simply not in his nature.

The old man explained that he and his daughter were not allowed to make contact, as part of the terms of the adoption. He then continued to explain, against his late daughter's wishes, that she suffered from Fatal Familial Insomnia.

"FFI is an extremely rare disease of the brain and can develop spontaneously," holding back his tears, he continued to explain that "it has no known cure and involves progressively worsening insomnia which leads to hallucinations, delirium, confused states like that of dementia, and eventually death. The average survival time once diagnosed is 18 months."

It has been found in just 40 families worldwide, affecting about 100 people. If only one parent has the gene, the offspring have a 50 percent risk of inheriting it and developing the disease. Commonly identified around middle age; this is why Steven's birthmother had to give him up. She knew she was a ticking time bomb and not fit to be around him.

The old man told Steven that it was considered essential that a potential patient be tested if they wish to avoid passing FFI on to their children, but his mother didn't want anybody living a life with a time limit or a fear of one.

"Now you have the information, Steven. Please respect your mother's wishes," said the old man.

The sadness of his earlier emotional trauma had instantly taken a back seat to this complete heavy load of information.

Flutters of joy that he was not abandoned by some drunk nobody as previously imagined, mixed with the fact that some crazy stranger had found him twice to try to give him some sort of estate.

"What exactly is this estate?" he asked with a tone that implied his interest was a favour or a burden to the old man.

His granddad revealed what was his prize to claim.

It was a six-bedroom house in West Yorkshire with savings worth up to 408,000 pounds.

You can imagine the confusion on Steven's face when receiving this information. Steven's adopted parents were by no means short of money, but this was perhaps in aid of the fact that they would not spend a penny too.

"And why did she have it and not you?" he asked.

"I have my demons and your mum had to help me through mine," Granddad says while sobbing. "No man should have to watch his baby girl die in such a degrading way and to watch her give you up. I lost too many things and didn't want to have anything to do with anything linked to her. I couldn't raise you and I'm sorry. I don't have long either, my son, and I will ride my days out in a hospice. If you want my advice…Don't find out…It is better to live before you die," he warned.

Steven called the old man a taxi and took him to his care home and promised to honour their wishes.

As the disappointed old man buckled up into the back seat, Steven shouted, "Let's meet up on Monday."

Chapter 3

Brian was the father of Steven's biological mum. He came from a long line of property developers in West Yorkshire but historical concessions and World War II impacted their portfolio deeply and at the time of Steven's birth, the estate was down to an old mill, which had been converted to apartments, a barn-house property and a modest sum of savings.

When Brian's daughter fell ill, it was all too quick for him to control or comprehend the emotional and financial downfall that he was to endure.

His only form of financial security was a proud standing stonewashed cotton mill that had been transformed into lavish luxury apartments on the canal bank of Todmorden. This site would be sold to ensure he could be a living carer for his daughter.

The confusion and fear in his altered path in life hit home when eight months prior he discovered that she was pregnant. Therefore, exercising his paternal instinct, he placed the barn house and savings in her name. This was also contributed by the knowledge that he had been diagnosed with cancer.

How does a dad react to cancer when he lost his wife years back? When his only daughter is carrying a child out of wedlock to a man that is untraceable?

His only instinct is to secure her future.

Brian told his daughter that he did this to be sensible about the future.

Then she fell ill. How does a man tell his precious little dinky that he may be checking out before her in the most scary and unanswerable moments of her life? He simply cannot! So, he did not.

He wanted her to believe there is a light at the end of the tunnel and so he hid his illness and he channelled all his love and energy into his daughter.

Brian was devastated that not only did his daughter get sick before his illness had evolved but by how quick and significant her condition would bypass and overdevelop in comparison to his cancer.

He never told his daughter about this because he expected to defeat it before it spread and as her problems and symptoms increased, he could never find it right in his heart to tell her. He had to be her rock.

Brian's daughter would find brief moments in her progressive decline where she was able to maintain normal conversations; and in these moments she would ask her father to raise her son as his own and ensure he was looked after. It was in one of these golden moments of normality that Brian would decline because he couldn't knowingly make the boy an orphan twice in a short period of time, still, he had to let his baby girl believe and know that it was because he was holding optimism for her recovery. This was clearly a lie, but he couldn't let her know that they were both on short time.

Brian's daughter would resent and eventually hate him for 'acting' like she would recover, even though he knew for certain that she in fact, would not.

In any parent's life, a dad never wants to outlive his kids, but he hated himself for fighting so hard to outlive her, only because he wanted to protect her until her last breath.

Once her condition was at its final point, Brian put Steven into care.

He used his highly expensive legal team to ensure that the situation regarding Steven was locked up in a strict 'ask no questions' type contact. He wanted to protect him from all the sadness that would unravel if he was to know where his roots would stem from.

He would sit by his daughter for her final weeks, watching the insanity, insomnia and schizophrenia eat her alive until she died from a heart attack one Valentine's morning.

Almost immediately, Brian retired to his late daughter's house and waited for cancer to take him like a swooshing wave from a Tsunami on a beachfront.

Steven's grandfather declined further treatment and would not attend any more appointments or consultations which added to his confusion and sadness when he discovered that it was taking too long to die.

It was only when the dead plants crisped over in his kitchen pots that he had realised that months had passed.

Only on this revelation, he entertained the idea of seeing his GP.

He was stunned to discover that his cancer had cleared.

Once he was satisfied that he was all clear, he would try to explain the situation to adoption authorities but due to the strict contract and conditions set out by him, he would never be able to track Steven's location.

Many years would pass and Brian would live as a recluse in the house, only leaving to walk alone or to visit a local cafe.

The locals would assume he was a drunk odd-ball because he would sit, not crying, but with tears silently falling to his chin, then to the floor as he gazed solemnly to an empty void.

Years passed and six months before Steven's 16th birthday, he was informed by his doctor that his cancer had returned and spread. He was dedicated to finding Steven so he paid an investigator to locate his family address, as he knew that once he was legally an adult, then he could make contact.

He had no desire or intent to meet Steven to fill him with tragedy or sadness but he wanted so badly to see him. It would be the final piece of his life's puzzle.

As soon as Brian gave Steven his note, he moved, unbeknown to Steven, in a nearby care home. Until their reunion one Halloween night, Brian would not bother Steven but he would silently observe him. Looking on him like a rebooted slideshow, rediscovering features, expressions, mannerisms and smiles that he only recognised as his late daughter's attributes.

His doctors were baffled by the way he battled to dominate his cancer. They could only place it down to Brian's immense heartbreak, tangled with his desire and need to know he settled his bets before he could leave this world.

Brian needed to know and wanted to know that Steven would take the house.

Not because he was worried that his estate would fall back into the system but that his bloodline may continue and that his only living relative would know who he was and where he came from.

In their short time, Seven and Brian slowly formed a bond. It was more of Steven listening to Brian's life before his mum, and him boasting of his accomplishments in a playful way that indicated clearly that his grandfather was in fact a humble man with no sense of entitlement despite his background.

They would play chess and walk around the city together, yet strangely ignore the elephant in the room, that was the wish, that was for Steven to move into the house. Steven never opposed it, but they were just content with being friends.

Steven would meet his granddad several times a week until Brian's time came. It was in his final moments that Steven eased his grandfather's mind by assuring him that he would go to West Yorkshire and live in his mother's family home.

When death met Brian, it was the first time he could recall feeling beautiful, free and wonderful, and he embraced his last moments as though he was boarding a plane to fly back home to his wife and beautiful baby girl.

Brian died peacefully in his sleep on a foggy Wednesday night.

Chapter 4

6 June 2004

The sound of a news reporter;

"Heads of state and thousands of war veterans gather in France to mark 60 years since D-Day. Queen Elizabeth II and 16 other leaders joined surviving veterans in the small seaside town to pay tribute to those who died spearheading the re-invasion of Nazi Europe 60 years before."

This was the report on the television news as Steven sat in the corner of his West Yorkshire caffe.

Quietly doing his books, he took a moment to lift his head and watch for a minute. He pushed his black-framed reading glasses up his nose as he smirked with the idea that his late granddad, whom he only knew for a short time, would always tell stories of how the media got the war wrong and how he could tell it right.

It had been three years and Steven was the proud owner of a little place directly in the middle of Manchester and Yorkshire. A rural place called Howorth, where he lived. Steven always hoped that he could convince Stephanie to come and work with him there. He would offer her the role of manager with the enticing promise of working what and when she wanted but she never took him up on his offer.

From time to time, she would come in and they would sit and talk for hours and he would almost make-believe that he was talking to his wife and every time she was about to leave, he would hold his arms out to hug her and she would come in from the side to give him a kiss on the cheek.

As Steven had re-immersed himself to his end of month stock counts, he saw in his peripheral a young lady hovering over. "Would you like more tea?" she stuttered.

"Diellza. How are you doing? I forgot it was your birthday," Diellza was a young Polish lady who applied to work for Steven a few months earlier.

Steven was reluctant to hire her because he couldn't pronounce her name. This was also the reason he felt obliged to offer her the job because he kept saying it wrong in her interview.

"Di-Yeh-Zah." He laughed as she told him previously that this is how it is pronounced.

"No thank you," he said smiling as he insisted she took the day off.

Diellza had only been in the country a short time. She had bottle-green eyes and short hair that was mousy brown.

When she spoke, she barely opened her mouth and she seemed to blink a lot, perhaps this was nerves but she always had a perfect posture with her back up straight. The tiny mole to the bottom of her nose and lips were so naturally pink that they looked like they had been drawn on by a makeup artist. She was extremely modest and wore very little makeup but she was pretty in such a subtle way.

She had impeccable manners, so much so that she would never accept tips from customers and even when her shift was finished, she would always stay and help if it was busy. She explained in her interview that she had come over to study to become a teacher. She and Steven would always exchange the same obligatory one-liners each day.

"More tea?"

"No, thank you."

Laugh at the poor pronunciation of name…quick "how is school?" …quick" okay" and that was it.

Nothing more, nothing less. She was quite scared of him because he was the boss and he was extremely uncomfortable by this because, in his eyes, this was all new to him. He had no sense of entitlement or feeling of deserving to his unknown mother's generosity. He just moved himself into her universe because he had no ties anywhere else in the world and living in her family home gave him a sense of family as though he actually came from real roots.

At the end of each day, Steven would take home whatever meal the ladies had made for the customers that day for tea, he would always stay just before closing time but would leave with enough time for the staff to cash up alone and lock up, this was his way of letting his staff know that he leads from the front when it comes to work ethics but also that he trusted them enough to handle the money and safety of the premises. This must have been something he had read in an idiot's guide to management.

When he got home each night he would walk through his huge kitchen and put the meal into the fridge. He never ate it, not for the lack of trust or respect but because he just wanted to get his generic bowl of chicken with Tabasco sauce and rice and speak with Stephanie.

Sometimes on the phone, sometimes by email or sometimes by text. But always and only if she was available. Sometimes he would message and wait hours, checking to see if she had responded. However, every night ended with his routine shower, shave, sit-ups and press-ups and the reading of his late birth mother's letter.

The house was beautiful. You could pass the turning on a country lane and never know it was there, but if by chance you took the 150-metre drive down the lane, then you would witness the immaculate 16th century farmhouse with a barn extension. The front of house driveway had a water fountain statue in the middle of the private roundabout, the old oak doors lead into a massive foyer with a staircase running both ways with a beautiful chandelier dominating the high wood beam ceilings. To the left was a library and to the right was the kitchen with huge stone tiled floors and an island in the middle with brass pans looming above.

The sinks were like baths and the oven was three times the size of any standard unit. Through the kitchen was a long hallway with another winding staircase at the end that leads to the master bedroom and through that door was a private bathroom.

This place was designed for a big family and it had a barn house that must have once been for staff.

The land stood modestly outback by a private lake that met with tall trees consuming the distant view.

The garden had a working well in the back and all kinds of stone carved monuments and run-down greenhouses and dying herb gardens.

The enormity of the house in its most grand spectrum gave no fulfilment to Steven. He just felt that this was where his mum wanted him to be and for no other reason he chose to stay there as this request was the only thing he ever really knew about her.

The house stood proud to an unassuming eye but was most certainly nobody's home any more. It was always tidy and well maintained but Steven had the same ritual. Come in, food in the kitchen, make fresh rice and chicken, go to bathroom, exercise, sit on the bed or by the desk in the bedroom and wait for Stephanie to love him back.

In every aspect of his life, he seemed calm, cool and collected but this was one spell that he was under and it was well and truly unbreakable.

One evening, whilst he was awaiting a response, he excitedly heard the buzz of his Motorola flip phone and he read with a familiar feeling of sting. Like a punch to the gut or the feeling of being a young boy, standing as you glide down a hill on your old BMX bike and as you swiftly take a seat and it slips down and you plummet to the middle bar of the bike and your whole body is rattled.

She has a boyfriend? Stephanie, the girl who doesn't want to be with anyone but if she did, it would be with a guy like Steven; with Steven's looks, personality, humour, good nature. If she was to be with anybody, it would be Steven. But no, she is with someone else.

His thoughts are red, his eyes are sore, his heart is bruised and his mind is florescent with colours, questions, sadness and rage.

"My fake parents hated me!"

"My mum's a coward! I'm stuck in a town I don't know, living a life that is not mine!" he yelled.

He is laughing, because he's pathetic, crying because he's laughing, nodding 'no' because he is laughing and crying and after a whirlwind of confusion and brainstorming, all of his responses and angry digs, witty remarks, planned comebacks after her preconceived comebacks, all the information he had ready and stored to get venomous and personal and he is about to do it. He is going to go insane and hit back. "The cheeky bitch played me for five years, using me? I'll show her."

As he starts all the letters

…Y…O…U…S…T…U…P…I…D…he starts to Delete

D<<<<< I<<<<<<< P<<<<<<

U<<<<<<<<T<<<<<<<S<U<O<Y

He deletes his rage, sits down and rubs his tired eyes as he has been waiting hours for his reply. He composes himself and exhales, "GOODBYE STEPHANIE." These were the only two words he allowed himself to use as his response.

Chapter 5

Christmas 2005

It was a frosty Wednesday morning and Steven had woken five minutes before his 6:30 alarm was set to go off, the cold room displayed much emphasis on his breath as he would not allow himself to heat his house, not because he was scared to spend, but simply because he felt a sense of guilt that he lived in such a fortunate postcode whilst there were others out there far worse off.

The thought of offering his spare rooms out had occurred to him on several occasions, but as there were so many grand artefacts and sentimental priceless objects from a family that he was clinging onto for some kind of identity, it meant he could not open himself up to trust a perfect stranger; needless to say he was understanding deeper and deeper each day, the extent to which the house was lacking living character.

He started to exercise his obligation to get to know the house a little more, so his route faded and from time to time, he would read in the library or tap the heavy white ivory keys on the enormous and heavy old upright piano, the twang of the middle C would bounce in pitch as it was aged and out of tune. He would walk out on to the slippery iced-up steps leading to the golden-brown flags in his back garden and sweep glue set leaves just to pass the time.

One particular morning, he looked into the large theatre dressing room style mirror in his bathroom, with a cheeky smile upon his face as he trimmed his recently grown beard. He began to smile because he recently had an ongoing joke with some of the ladies who worked with him.

There were three ladies who worked in his café, who had worked there for many years under the previous owners who sold to Steven so that they could emigrate to Alicante.

These ladies had managed to break through his private barrier and managed to squeeze in a few slight moments where he would drop his quiet and polite façade and sometimes catch himself enjoying the harmless back and forth of playful words.

Joyce was in her early 60s and refused to retire. She had known Steven's mum but she was a traditional lady and would not gossip or small talk, so although she may have wanted Steven to intrude on his boundaries and ask more, she respected that he never did. She would simply capture the odd moment to relate her to a nice memory, like identifying his soft nature as a kind gift handed to him by her.

Barbara was Joyce's sister-in-law, and they bickered all the time but loved each other like real sisters. She would complain that Joyce would take hours making the cheese and onion pie upstairs, whilst she was round the front holding the fort, but secretly loved the feeling of being needed. It was common practice for the locals to tell them both to put a sock in it when their bickering soured a little more than their usual playful back and forth, but as soon as and if anyone would rein them in, they would joint attack their opponent like an unbreakable team.

Kathy was a few years younger than Joyce and Barbara, but she was the sensible one. She would always observe everybody and their behaviour, she would nudge Diellza to

Steven's table, or interrupt a conversation when she saw that people were uncomfortable.

The three of them were best friends and went to bingo every Tuesday night. Their love was the cafe. They all considered going into partnership and buy the place when it came on the market. They were devastated when they heard some young hotshot beat them to it and purchased it and they took a dislike to Steven before they met him, but in their first encounter with him, they knew he was a good man, and instantly found a fondness for him.

So, two days before the Monday they managed to get Diellza to dare him to shave off his beard.

He always took Tuesdays off, and so his smile was that he felt like he had a tiny victory in keeping it. It was at this moment that he realised two things…

1) He realised that he started to enjoy his life in West Yorkshire and 2) He needed a housekeeper to run his house so that it always had a living soul in the property to feel that it was home as opposed to a lonely yet beautiful house.

Chapter 6

Baaa Dooop! went the electrical bell to the shop door. It was one of those tiny white boxes over the door that made a two-syllable Baa Doop as it opened.

The staff there hated it because for years they had an old brass cowbell and it felt rural and real, but their fondness for Steven and the fact that it was the only change he had made to the cafe meant it would never be complained about.

The shop was very busy, especially considering it had been one of the coldest days of the season; it was lovely and warm once inside, as it was important to him that all staff and customers felt toasty and warm in his cafe, the only time it felt cold was when the wind flew in sharply like it had been sent through on a perfectly folded paper aeroplane, as the door would open with the 'on cue' Baa Doop!

Smiling as they would roll the pastry for the lunchtime pie with the white towel thrown over their right shoulders, there were the three ladies, they all cupped their hands and rubbed their chins to signal that he was adamant with keeping his beard. Joyce playfully dusted a fingers brush of flour on Steven's cheek.

"How are we doing guys? Very busy for a Wednesday?" he said with pride.

Looking around he noticed Diellza was not there, after questioning one of the ladies in the kitchen it was brought to his attention that she had not been in on the previous day also.

This was extremely out of character for Diellza, as in the last year she had become a welcomed member of the community, still very shy and very nervous and always reluctant to speak to Steven about anything unrelated to work, yet highly regarded as a perfectly polite lady.

It was very much out of character for Steven but he felt the impulse to go and visit her at home as he knew she had no family.

He wanted to be sure she was okay and ensure his worst thoughts were as bizarre as they sounded when he said them under his breath…

"What if she is dead on her floor?"

"What's that, Steve?" asked Barbara, looking over her lenses that looked like huge NHS supplied glasses from the later 70s.

"Nothing," he rushed, as he left through the door.

Baa Doop!

Pulling halfway up the hill in the little village of Mytholmroyd, he left his Black Mondeo at the end of the road as the houses were so tight and narrow that he would have not been able to turn round. The huge bulky stone bricks on the tall standing two-bedroom terrace houses awaited Steven's tired feet as all of the steps to each door were 15 rows high in concrete slabs.

The house had netted curtains and a 'To Let' sign being hammered into the four-foot patch of frozen grass by an estate agent's handyman.

On asking this man where Diellza had gone to, he was informed that she had been evicted and had to be gone by close of business that day, so Steven sat on the cold step for well over three hours, getting up every now and then to wake his tired sleeping legs.

Not far off eleven o'clock, she came to the house to collect her final bits to load into her old Silvery Blue Volvo, she masterfully reversed parked right up to the house.

"Steven," gasped Diellza.

"Can we go inside, Diellza? After all, it is still your house for six more hours, isn't it?" he pleaded as he stepped aside, shivering.

Diellza opened the door trying to contain her shaking chin as her bottom lip rattled with the combination of the shattering cold air and her composure that was inevitably about to go.

Her empty boxes that she had brought ready to load had not managed to hit the ground before she sobbed into her fluffy brown woolly gloves.

Steven picked her up straight away without a word muttered and just hugged her until the crying faded out, the sustained moan emptied in volume like a vacuum cleaner that had just been switched off until it faded into a few sniffles and coughs, and she pulled away from the un-seemingly comfortable hug and pushed him away lightly as she offered him a hot drink.

The clock had spun right to 1:15 in what seemed like minutes, Diellza explained to Steven that she had been struggling to keep up with her rent and bills, things had escalated so poorly that she had to leave night school and fight to break even for so long.

She continued to open up about how she was not technically in the UK as a citizen so she could not seek help from the government as she feared she would be sent home.

Sobbing she went deeper into her distress and explained that she was not actually a Polish Immigrant and in fact she was Albanian.

She managed to smuggle herself to the UK under very dangerous and risky conditions.

Illegal immigrants from Albania and Ukraine were trafficked into Britain by devious crooks who would train them to act Polish. Diellza put herself in the most life-threatening situation hiding on a ferry that she knew was linked to illegal trafficking gangs just to flee her country, she would not tell Steven what was so bad that she would endanger her entire life to leave but he knew it was something that she locked away in her mind and so he respected that.

By two o'clock Steven managed to settle Diellza. They joked that this was probably the most they had spoken in the 18 months they had known each other. Steven made a personal request to Diellza.

"Please come and work directly for me? I need a Housekeeper," he explained.

Diellza looked unsure of Steven's intentions so he swiftly protected his integrity as he emphasised that he wants a strictly professional relationship, she would live in the property and basically run the house.

He noted that since his residency began, no plant had been watered, no pan used and in fact not one square meal had been made, Steven was tidy and clean but he would not go into many rooms and so light fittings had cobwebs, some light switches had not even been switched on, it was a lonely house and he wanted somebody to run it for him.

Diellza accepted this arrangement even though a large part of her instincts told her he was creating this situation out of the kindness of his heart and not for his convenience.

As a final request, he asked if he could drive the Volvo home. He said it was his adoptive dad's car growing up and that he wanted to drive it, she knew this was definitely a lie and that he was just being noble and wanted to let her drive to Howorth in his warm heated car.

With the last few boxes in both cars, they each drove down the hill into the valley. Diellza followed Steven as she left Mytholmroyd without even a slight glance through the rear-view mirror.

Pulling up to the roundabout at the end of the narrow secret lane, Diellza was in complete shock at the beauty that stood before her.

She got out of the car and scrunched her eyes together until she saw the pink and red lining in the skin of her eyelids, then blinked rapidly and opened them wide.

Explaining to a very confused-looking Steven, she shared a memory as a child and that whenever her eyes saw new beauty she would do this process because the end result adds a perfect brightness to her vision and so, to her, she believed that what is in front of her is in fact real and not a dream and felt like the flash from a photo that she would add to her mind's album.

"Leave the bags, Diellza, let me show you around and show you your room," he ushered.

Diellza fell in love with the building but contained this emotion as she didn't know how long this arrangement would last and she didn't want to encourage any misconception that she had any interest in taking advantage of Steven in any way.

But she knew in her heart that this place was a place of her dreams and she could not wait to get settled in.

Steven explained that he gave her complete creative freedom of the house, his only request was anything of sentiment to his family remain a feature.

Diellza asked very timidly, "Would you mind awfully if I cleaned the curtains?"

"Absolutely not! I hope you don't judge but I have not made this place a home and I want you to do exactly that. Please wake the old lady up," Steven remarked, smiling he passed her a debit card, he told her this could be seen as the company credit card and she could purchase groceries, fuel, and anything that she considered necessary to the upkeeping of the house.

This was not usually the kind of trust Steven had invested in anybody but there was the sinister joker card which was that she had nowhere or nobody to go to and he had found himself, as others did, to like and respect her over the last two years.

"What about the café?" she asked.

"You can work shifts there too so you are not stuck in one place all day? Nobody needs to know anything about your eviction," he replied.

There was still a very closed-off dialogue between them, perhaps heightened now as Steven didn't want to appear to mislead her into thinking there was anything more than an arrangement and Diellza could not change her view on her boss being her boss.

Diellza accepted the cafe position but requested to work the two days where Steven is not there, her intention was so that he can enjoy his home time alone.

A few days had passed and Steven returned home from the café. Pulling up to the driveway, he instantly noticed the fresh new curtains on all of the front windowpanes.

This made Steven breathe in a very ecstatic smile. He switched off the ignition and walked in. Before entering the kitchen, he could smell a combination off banana skin, lavender and garlic. Again he smiled but before he opened the door he cleared the smile, it was vital to him that she saw him as an employer and not a friend so he walked in, fairly stern, but there was nobody there, the table was made up for one and there was a bowl of fresh fruit in the basket that previously had unread mail in it; in the windowsill was a lavender plant and on the oven was a homemade lasagne.

On the table there was a note which informed Steven that she had gone to see if she could enrol into her teaching class again, her intention was to leave him in peace, she didn't think it was appropriate to eat with him.

This would happen for many months, each night with a different excuse…

Beef Wellington followed by a note saying Diellza was at the gym…

Cottage Pie followed by a note saying Diellza was revising at the local college library…

Shepherd's pie followed by a note saying Diellza was at the gym…

Chilli Con Carne…Swimming

Curry with rice…Gym

Salad…Shopping

Pork Chops…College

And so on.

Even Christmas Day she would refuse to go with Steven to his annual obligatory, defrosted from frozen, roast dinner with his adoptive father.

Into the new year as the winter withdrew, she would take up running. Steven would come home to a different meal, and over time he would notice things like flower baskets hanging in front of the house or the revised home-grown herb farm by the back window, the statue in the roundabout on the drive was of stone, jet-washed, and the little angel was actually spitting out a real flow of water.

His laundry always smelt of a spring meadow and his clothes were so perfectly pressed that he looked as though his shirts were drawn on when he wore them.

His bedding was always fresh and turned and he would never know what the beautiful scent was, but his bathroom was so opal fresh that he would smell candles in shops and products in the local grocery store to try to identify and recreate this euphoric aroma.

Without realising it, he had a wonderfully beautiful, perfect home, and it looked great, smelt great, felt great; it was great.

It was a running living home and he loved it.

Upon arriving at this conclusion, he also realised that he barely ever saw Diellza. She became an expert at presenting the dream home and staying out of his way. They were by no means rude, but they were strangers in the house and Steven wanted to try his best to make her feel that she didn't always have to hide. He was unsure how to approach this without coming across as too full on.

It was June 3rd, and a 26-year-old Steven was ready for Diellza to come back from college, and he was going to suggest something that would break the ice whilst ensuring it is taken as a platonic gesture. So he had an idea to play chess. Yes, chess. The least romantic, least exciting, least entertaining of all games to allow for some conversation and interaction.

As he heard the high revs of her tatty Volvo, he came to the door to let her in to tell her what he wanted to do in order to make her feel at home.

Before he could speak, she bluntly exclaims, "Steven, I have to go home!"

This time in complete control, like a matter of fact, something that Steven thought, if ever, would be delivered with floods of tears.

She explained that by enrolling into her course for teaching, it led to them doing something called a CRB check and a DBS check which looked into an individual's background and history. When asked by the staff at college, she was hesitant and so after them investigating it they checked her files, applications and details and notified the local council.

She was accepting of the matter because there was simply no hiding or escaping it. The council had notified the authorities.

"Tell them we are engaged," Steven spurted, holding his top lip as though he wasn't controlling his words as he muttered them.

"Absolutely not," she insisted. "And please, Steven, don't for one second think I even thought of this, I am not a gold digger, and I am not prepared to do that," she continued.

The conversation continued with Steven presenting his case as Diellza would reject each offer that Steven would throw out. It was like a verbal game of chess.

Steven showed a moment's weakness for the first and only time since she had met him and he stressed that it would be her doing him the favour.

His house had never been so homely, he had a lovely home growing up but he had immense lack of communication with people he lived with, nothing like all the wonderful things she brought to this home.

He opened up so much whilst still visibly holding himself at arm's length and keeping up a secure guard.

He talked about his confusing background. He was very frank about the fact that he had no desires towards Diellza whatsoever and told her of his undying love for Stephanie, he explained how every song he listened to takes him to a memory of them, even still when he would hear a joke he would demonstrate smiling as though he was right there in the fantasy…

"It's her I want to tell it to…I smell her perfume in the shop and I look up in hope it is her. I am head over heels in love with her and she feels nothing for me," he confessed lowering his shoulders and dropping his arm's length guard.

He made it so evidently clear that he just didn't want to lose such a good employee that he was willing to marry her to keep her in the country.

Truly believing that he was sincere she accepted his offer. On the one condition that she signs to say that if anything happens, then she is not entitled to a penny of his estate. She was adamant about this. His final condition would be that they at least eat dinner together at night.

They travelled up to Scotland and married in a small village. Just the two of them. They had a locally cooked meal and shared a dance, there was zero romance there but a long smile that congregated a sincere level of respect and understanding for each other.

When returning, they shook hands and went off into their own rooms.

After the marriage, Diellza stopped working her shifts at the cafe, not as to hide anything but they both respected the three ladies and so didn't want to be in a position where they would appear dishonest or deceitful.

They made their arrangement and there was no reason it couldn't work.

Chapter 7

It was the one-year wedding anniversary. Both Steven and Diellza were pretending like they were unaware because if they said they knew, then it would be a form of celebrating it which would be assuming it mattered more than the arrangement but a card from the little Scottish village of Gretna Green meant they have to address it.

The last 12 months had been the perfect working relationship.

Steven had even pulled away from the cafe to help Diellza farm her hens and convert the back garden into an allotment where she grew fresh vegetables.

They struggled for a while to really talk any deeper than pleasantries but on this day when watering the grass, he playfully splashed her with the hose and so later on when his back was turned, and he was digging out weeds she threw a rotten tomato at him then turned away as though it wasn't her. They were both loosening up and slowly becoming friends.

Diellza made a handcrafted sign at the end of the lane telling passers-by that they sold fresh eggs and this meant that they would get to know their neighbours a little more.

She managed to secure herself a placement as a teaching assistant which meant they shared the running of the house, but Steven loved this.

He felt like this was the reason his mum wanted him to move here, almost as if she knew that if he embraced it, it would bring out his better self. He never realised how much he loved the outdoors.

Further up the lane was a steep hill that Diellza and Steven would walk up, right to the top they would climb and at its highest point was a bench and you could see the Three Valleys. Steven loved the evening breeze in his face and Diellza enjoyed his smile when he was taking in the majestic view.

For their first anniversary, they agreed to have a lasagne. The first meal Diellza ever made for Steven. This time they would enjoy it together.

"We have post for the Mr and Mrs," Diellza boasts sarcastically.

"The guys at the cafe I'm guessing," assumed Steven.

Diellza opened the letter and leaves it on the table as she excused herself and walked away to her room.

Looking very confused, Steven read the letter. The letter from Stephanie.

To the happy Couple.

Oh my God, I can't believe my best friend found the love of his life.

I can't believe I had to find out from the staff in your cafe but I wish you both a very happy ever after.

P.S Not all people are bad. Sometimes good people just get things wrong.

I hope you are well and I'm so happy you are happy.

Love Stephanie.

Temporarily dismissing the letter Steven tended to Diellza's reaction.

Knocking on her door Steven rambled through the solid oak.

"Why is this bothering you? We are not a married, married couple?" scrunching his lips as he pulled his cheekbones in as though he has a tangy-sweet in his mouth.

"The fact that you do not understand is why I do not want to talk about it," Diellza firmly responded.

With little understanding of the situation, Steven left her alone.

In her room, Diellza was looking at pictures that they had taken on the wedding day, these photos were taken at the time to prove that they were in fact married if ever questioned. She was drawing her finger around Steven in the sad realisation that she was in fact in love with him.

She had been feeling this way for some time; her confidence as a lady had grown, her strength as a teaching assistant had evolved beyond her wildest expectations and she had loved having Steven to herself, never really needing to address it prior to Stephanie's letter, she managed to even fool herself to believe that this could last forever. She was not scared to lose the house or the financial security, she didn't want to lose him.

Chapter 8

As the fallen leaves turned to a combination of pond green and caramel gold, the crisp air had tightened, and Diellza and Steven were almost strangers in the same home.

The once happy moving mechanism of the house had halted its spin and the charm from within had diminished.

Diellza was still true to her word and so, fresh meals were placed on the table each night, the house immaculate, lavender pouring out in its scent through the corridors into each room and without fail; the house stood proud in its presentation, only without their tailor-made friendship sustaining its glory.

Steven receded back into his protective bubble and Diellza didn't intrude on his behaviour.

One chilly evening, they were both settling themselves at each end of the house when a ferocious rumble echoed through the bricks.

The zip and zap and strike of the sharpest flash from an enchanting blue bolt of lightning shone through Diellza's window, splitting the weeping willow outside, into pieces. It lit up the sky long enough for her to observe the blackest of clouds in the distance.

The thunder was as though ancient demigods were wrestling in the mountains, launching car-sized rocks beside them as they rough it out and Diellza was petrified from her 'ring-side' view.

She screamed with fear as the lights and all power in the house went out with a bang. She was in complete darkness. The kind of darkness where you would doubt your own senses if you were to wave your own hands in front of your face.

Covered in her bedsheets she saw a bright yellow line right under the crease of her bedroom door followed by a knock!

"Are you OK, Diellza?" asked Steven.

"I'm fine," she stuttered, followed by another blast of thunder.

She screamed again. "I'm coming in," he warned. Creaking through the door with an old candle-lit lantern and a silver Parker pen with a white flannel hanging over it.

"I have plenty of candles in the kitchen and plenty of wine. I surrender my white flag," he joked.

Diellza smiled and removed herself from the fortress of pillows and followed Steven to the kitchen.

As Steven realised that this was not only the first time he had genuinely socialised with Diellza, it was also the first time he had known her to be completely at ease in his company. Diellza was so relaxed and her comfort oozed with a boom of confidence that Steven saw within her. He aligned her confidence and comfort with blissful beauty and it was then that he began to see what had been in front of him all this time.

Hours into the night and the wine was flowing like velvet; and the sounds of the storm had turned into trickling showers which presented themselves in a form of musical background sounds.

Diellza and Steven were laughing once more.

From solitaire to chess to connect four, they would find many pointless pastimes to pass the time.

By which time the old grandfather clock in the library let them know it was one o'clock in the morning with its confident 'BOING'.

They upgraded to brandy and threw logs on the fire, mocking at the fact that they were drinking brandy merely because it felt like something wealthy people should do in a home-built library, they joked and laughed.

Placing her glass down and pulling the cuffs of her sleeve over her thumb to warm up more, she leans forward and looks to Steven; ready to be intrusive in intrigue for the first time since they met.

Steven, noting her increased chill, throws more logs onto the fire as he anticipates, "Go on! Ask me anything you want," Steven challenges, watching eagerly.

"It would be so rude of me to ask, but I wouldn't be human if I didn't wonder," she explained.

Steven shimmered his rocking chair closer to Diellza's chair and put his arm on the arm of her chair, in a way that opened his body language without physical contact.

"Ask me anything and everything Diellza," he said as he sipped the large glass of brandy.

"Well then, Steven. Tell me everything and anything, because I simply know nothing…Mr Husband," she grinned.

For the first time in Steven's life, he was absolutely happy to tell his story, from beginning to end he explained it all, his estranged grandfather, his adoptive parents, his loss and love and his yearning to learn about his real mother, his love for Stephanie.

This was what took most of his time, but he didn't hold back, by the end of his two-hour tale, she almost rooted for him to win Stephanie one day, solely based on his intense unconditional devotion to his heart's desire when it came to her existence.

He talked and she listened and at no point did she interrupt or draw away. She smiled as the flaming logs turned into cinders looking at the love he had for her.

She felt a dint in her heart when he talked of his family and she felt a solid respect growing deeper within when she realised that this is a man who sincerely asks for nothing from anybody else, though he will surrender himself for others. She knew she was falling deeper for him, but his story was bigger than her, so she was able to mask it well this time.

"Let's do you now," Steven said with a tipsy slur as he slammed the empty glass down.

"Excuse me!" laughs Diellza as she put her empty glass down.

Steven goes to pour another, but she politely declines, as she indicates by moving the glass further away from the side table.

Steven continues, "Tonight belongs to the storm so we can bare all. No restrictions. Tell me more about DI-YE-ZA!"

Moving the glass back towards her she raised her eyebrows to request a final top-up. Steven poured the final drips of the dusty brandy bottle and poured them a last glass.

"The words I say now are going to be heard for the first time as and when they leave my tongue and I'm already scared to bring them to life. Though you have been brave to me, Steven, so I will pay you the same respect," she warned.

Sitting back into the brown leather chair, he massaged the golden buttons that pinned the fabric to the wood and waited for her to begin.

Diellza told Steven of the horrific scenes she witnessed as a child.

Her father was a drunk named Altin. He would come home at any hour on the clock and viciously beat her mother.

Her mother was a beautiful lady who worshipped him and took him back on so many occasions. She was the youngest of two sisters and one brother, she was graciously feminine in her ways and wonderfully loyal to her husband. She would stand by his side through thick and thin and they met difficult times financially, but she always ensured there was food on the table. Her most notable trick was to lay fresh lavender on the bedding to make the sheets smell fresh in her room. She just wanted a perfect happy home with a loving husband; however, she would become increasingly jealous that her husband was able to love Diellza and care so much for her, yet he could not show love to her. He would burn his wife with his cigars, throw plates at her if he didn't like the food she prepared and finally towards the end of everything he would invite men round at different times.

Diellza explains that as a child all she took in was the closing of a door if her peering eyes took note of such events, it was only as she got older that she knew what was going on.

One day after school she described how she was asking about her Daddy, but Mummy said he had gone to work away and that they were staying at Diellza's uncle's house. Her mother's older brother.

She loved to stay there growing up. It was in Poland. Out in the countryside about 30 miles south of the main city, they lived in a cottage by acres of grass.

They would go for short breaks on the very few occasions they were lucky enough to afford as a family and the views were magnificent.

This was her favourite place in the entire world. This little cottage stood modestly amongst a huge woodland, and she felt so safe here, and so did her mother. So, this particular day when she came home, she was thrilled to learn she was going there with her mummy. She didn't question why her daddy was away even though she had a feeling that her mummy was erratic and out of character.

Her mother hurried her and they got into her friend's car and was about to drive off when Altin appeared in front of the rusty bonnet of the car. The man driving the car shot off and was never seen again and her daddy told Diellza to stay sat in the car.

He and her mummy went into their apartment, and she knew from the drawn-out look in her mummy's eyes that something was up.

Diellza could hear bangs and crashes and smashes and knocks and she locked the car doors and put her thumbs in her ears and turned them to muffle out the noises.

She explained that it felt like hours that she sat in the car and it was only when the night came in that she ran out of the car over the stones and straight to her bedroom.

In bed at night, she heard crying from her mummy, cries of distraught, pain, fear, and emptiness; then she would hear what she later learnt was the sound of her parents having sex, then more tears.

The next day Diellza woke up and her daddy was sat with a bottle of Raki, a very strong clear liquor that is distilled from the dregs left after wine is pressed from grapes, she wouldn't know until days later that he was drinking first thing because his wife ran away hours earlier.

Sobbing, Diellza continued her story.

Altin became a ghost in their home. Diellza fed herself and took herself to school. Altin would work, come home and drink Raki looking at the door. The man that adored her was gone.

She hated her mummy for this as she thought it was her fault that her daddy no longer loved her. Although she knew her mummy had been treated wrong, she also knew that whilst this was the case, she was abandoned and therefore she was angry. This routine was in place for several years until Diellza transformed into a young lady.

One night in bed she heard Altin come home yelling, "Diellza!" at the top of his voice. She instantly pretended to be asleep.

She heard his steel toe cap thuds as he pounded up the stairs and she felt a real fear. "Diellza," the louder cry rang.

The door was open and through her squinted eyes she saw a blurred outline of her father with a tatty vest and gut hanging out with his belt and top two buttons undone.

"Are you awake girl," Altin mumbled.

Diellza just squashed her eyes tight and tensed her whole body. Fearing the worst, she tried to tighten the flaky grey sheets closer to her to act as a shield.

Altin took his yellow-brown corduroy pants off and lay next to her in the bed. To her complete repulsion, he threw his heavy body behind hers, stinking of alcohol and making her feel utter rage with his skin on hers; then he fell flat asleep. His beard was like wet wire and smelt like the iron elements in dry blood.

Diellza knew in her heart of hearts that had he believed she was awake, then she would have replaced the horrible void which her mother once filled.

It was at this moment that she realised she didn't blame her mother for running. She didn't sleep or move the whole night, instead, she cried silently through fear he would wake and act on his foul instincts.

Diellza knew that she had to leave the next day and snuck onto a cargo ship that she believed had ladies set to traffic aboard, she took her chances and never looked back.

As she stood from the chair, she walked over to Steven's vestibule and took out another bottle of Brandy. This was the only time she ever took a single item without asking in front of him, she opened the cap and drank a swig from the bottle.

"To Altin, you filthy pig," she toasted as she gulped and spat it out into the dead fire causing a flash of ember.

Diellza then fell into Steven's arms as he quickly stood to catch her fall. She cried into his neck as he pulled her chin up. Steven wiped the tear falling from her right eye and drew it back up to the corner of her eye.

They glanced into one another, unlike any other moment between their intoxicated game of romanced chess but still knowing a sincere sense of understanding for the loneliness they had both endured.

This was not a pitiful stare, just an acknowledgement that they were lost until they made the arrangement.

Five BOINGS on the grandfather's clock snapped them out of the trance they found themselves into which Steven insisted, "I'll walk you to your room, Diellza."

As they were walking down the hall, they found that their merry stagger had guided Steven's arm around Diellza's shoulder. As the corridor became too narrow to walk side by side, Diellza took an extra step forward which caused Steven's hand to slide away from her. As his hand fell, her right arm glided backwards and his left hand caught her fingers to keep the contact. The fingers pulled in and they were holding hands. At her door, she hugged him as though they found their friendship again and she thanked him for an amazing evening. Diellza then retired to her room.

Steven waited outside the door for a minute, stroking his chin, looking to the ceiling and with the tip of his toe, he pushed the door open.

Diellza was lifting her shirt over her head as she turned to see him. Normally she would cower and hide but she gave him the opportunity to react.

Steven stood and watched her. Diellza faced forward knowing he was watching and unhooked her bra as she dropped it to her side. She then unbuttoned her black jeans and let them fall to the floor.

Turning all the way around, she stood and stared deep into Steven's eyes and without taking the glance away she locked on to him. He in turn could not remove his eyes from her eyes. As they were having the perfect standoff, she put each thumb into the waistline of her black underwear and pushed as she let them drop to the ground. Diellza then turned away and climbed beneath the sheets.

Steven was stood in awe; the cold chill of the waking morning began to glimmer through the curtains and the alcohol was thinning his blood and he felt an exciting live anxious confusing urge to stay. He paused, then turned to the door. He paused again and turned right back around. He removed his clothes as he entered her bed.

Chapter 9

Winter

Steven was behind the counter at his cafe and was getting yelled at by an extremely vile and aggressive man.

This man had a large red nose with wide-open pours glaring off the greasy side of it and shaving cuts all over his face with two small angel wings tattooed on the side of his neck.

Moments earlier, the lady accompanying him claimed that there was a strand of hair on her food despite eating nearly all of the dish. Steven, knowing the routine that had been presented to him on so many occasions, though it would be easier to refund her meal.

They were not local faces, so he gathered they were just passing through and chancing their luck.

Once the man realised how quick Steven was to refund, he was demanding a refund for his plate also and asking for a gesture of goodwill for the inconvenience. Furious at Stevens declining him, he was getting louder and more offensive.

"Calm it boy," said a huge stranger.

This man had black hair and arms that looked like legs.

He carried a weight full of a gut but was clearly a strong looking fella.

The obnoxious man responded, "Shut it, old man!"

The huge stranger stood up and as he pulled from his chair, his torso didn't appear to stop. He was gigantic.

He walked towards the spiteful couple slowly and they muttered fearful shimmers under their breath and left the cafe without a further threat.

"Thank you," Steven said, "please have another coffee on the house."

This man had been in and out of the cafe for a few weeks. He would come in, order black coffee and a croissant, sit quietly but eagerly look around from the top of his newspaper from time to time.

"I'm grateful for the offer but it's no problem, sir. I just hate bullies," he modestly rejected in a very low-toned broken English accent.

He then put his five-pound note on the counter and left.

Hours would pass and Steven was getting in the way of the three ladies.

He had been hiding in the cafe for over a month, avoiding Diellza because he felt he had crossed a line with her.

They had this wonderful night and yet they had become like strangers once again. Still pleasant and polite, smiling as they pass in the halls but equally they both still felt a detraction in their mannerisms since the blackout.

The ladies told Steven to go home so he followed their request.

Pulling into the driveway the car slivered left to right over the ice-topped stones.

Steven looked through the windscreen to see two very strange things. The first is that all of the curtains were closed and all the lights were off as though Diellza has stood up and left.

His heart amplified with an involuntary thud and the silent squeaking noise howled through his ears with instant worry.

The second thing that confused him as he brought his senses back to ground was the strange old man sitting on the door. It was the man from the cafe.

He sat with a skin-coloured suede coat, the shiniest brown shoes and a hat that looked as though it belonged to an upper-class gentleman's club in 1912.

Steven got out of the car and the old man rushed to his feet and before Steven could ask why he was here, the man held both hands out, the right hand shook Steven's hand firmly whilst the left hand covered his other hand to cup Steven's hand. He then pulled him in. Steven could only focus on how huge these hands were.

"You are the good man from the Cafe! Are you my darling Diellza's husband?" he said. Steven, whilst still holding onto his right hand, loosened his grip and pushed him away slightly.

"You are the dad?" Steven asked.

Thinking on his feet he continued, "Diellza is away for the weekend but if you leave your details, I will get her to call you," he assured as he used his still shaking hand to manoeuvre Altin away from the door and into the direction of the driveway.

"We will be sure to call you in the next few days," said Steven whilst giving him a look that confirmed that Altin's reputation had been made known to him. Steven held a look into Altin's eyes that was enough to show that he was not a polite little pushover, but Altin knew Steven was startled.

Altin smiled as he tilted the tip of his hat down and bid Steven good night.

"Good night, Altin," Steven offered with a protective reluctance.

As the huge oak door slammed, Steven looked to the top of the staircase and saw Diellza on the top step.

Her elbows resting on her kneecaps as her palms covered her trembling face. She had been crying in dark silence from the moment she saw him walk down the driveway. He had been waiting there for two hours and she was too afraid to even move.

"Diellza. Come here," he cried out.

Diellza ran to him and he held her for what felt like ten minutes. She exploded in volume from a two-hour silenced fear and buried her head into Steven's shoulders.

On the other side of the hug Steven was holding in his trembling lips. Steven dismissed the twitch on his left nostril as he didn't understand the flood of emotion that took over his body in moments where he felt Diellza's fear and pain.

He just held her until she was ready to stop.

Steven then took Diellza's hand, there was not a word muttered as he stroked his thumb into her soft tiny palm. Her fingers would form a cup over his thumb as they walked, their hearts were beating and they were talking in body language, the words that were not being said were clear as day. The understanding that when one hurts, the other bruises. When one is scared, the other makes it okay, when one is sad, the other holds the door shut and keeps the bad things away.

Walking down the hallway, it's as though they are gliding. They arrive at Steven's door. He brushes it open with his left hand and guides her through with his right hand still holding her. He gently pushes the door shut with his left hand then places it on her ribs as he stands behind her.

Diellza has her eyes closed and is incomplete tranquillity as one cold tear escapes her right eye. Steven moves his hand up her body and down her arm as he floats his hands over to her right cheek like a feather. He gently turns her head to face him and once again he wipes the lonely tear away. A routine none of them want to keep reliving but it is the moments of utter hurt where Steven appears to let his heart lead his head.

He freezes for a moment then blinks. They are not even sure if they are holding hands anymore as they are hallucinating in a place where only they know, where the language is one that only they speak. He gulps and blinks as he thinks about kissing her and as he opens his eyes from the short fast flickered blinking, he feels her lips on his. Her lips feel cold but taste like strawberry. The kiss is so delicate and light that they still feel air-bound.

Diellza scrapes her nails through the back of Steven's hair and pulls him in, Steven picks Diellza up by digging his fingertips into the bottom of her thighs and he lays her down to the bed. She shimmers on up to the top of the bed as she watches him undress and their eyes are once again locked!

Steven crawls up the bed to meet her kiss once more as their hand's grip, he then scratches his way down her underarms; she waves her arms up in the air so that he can pull off her top. As her cold body is left unclothed, her hands go to her side as she pulls down her pants, at the same time he is taking off her bra and kissing the side of her breast ensuring there is no part of her upper body that is not being kissed.

He moves his mouth to her torso and kisses her belly button. As he takes her underwear down to her knees, not missing out her ankles as he kisses her thigh, shin and feet as he pulls the final part away from her right leg. He looks over her in her full naked beauty and gulps again. He worships her and he needs her to feel this worship physically. Her beauty had been missed by so many people, her eyes are wide open with lashes that look like an artist has sculptured them, her nose goes thin at the end and looks like it's always cold and her cheeks have bumps in them that look like her face is designed to smile more. He looks at her and she pulls him in.

Steven is making love to Diellza so slow and passionate. It's like it is his first time and he is so frightened that he will hurt her that he is completely gentle. His infatuation for her navigates him to embrace and relish every moment and every touch.

Her pelvis is lifting each time he thrusts himself upon her, she is feeling every emotion he has in his body as they say no words. Diellza has never felt more confident and safer than this exact moment so she takes the lead a little bit and turns him over from above her as she gets on top of Steven. Slowly gyrating him she holds his tight chest and guides his hands to her breasts as her nipples are so erect that she wants him to feel them. Steven places his hand round her neck and pulls her head towards him as they pick up the pace. He holds her left bottom cheek as he pulls her towards him as she thrusts down and there is now music in their unspoken language; like Samuel Barber's *Adagio for strings* as all the music changes from a peaceful melodic climb into a squelching bombardment of high-pitched strings, and it's climbing and growing as Diellza is moaning with utter euphoria. Steven is panting and trying to contain his excitement; and in the final moments, Diellza draws her back so far that her hands meet Steven's feet and she holds them. Her pelvis begins to lift and so does Steven's thighs until his bottom is elevated off the bed and Diellza is lifted higher inside of Steven and they fall to an exhausted kiss.

Lying in Steven's arms they both look up, still in silence, using their gripped hands to make shadow puppets against the wall aided by the chink in the curtain and the Victorian street lantern-style lamp post that is outside glaring through. Steven kisses Diellza's forehead and they fall asleep in each other's arms with the delicate sheets barely covering them.

The next day and even the next few weeks are like a dream. Diellza and Steven are there.

They are like giggling school children messing around and flirting and leaving notes for each another.

Diellza never called her father back, even though he left several messages and letters; he did not call at the house. He must have seen a protective shield within Steven's eyes when he shook his hand that day.

Altin did still visit the cafe on a regular basis; coffee croissant and paper and was always very polite to Steven and all the staff but he would never ask or mention anything about that visit until Steven approached him.

Steven and Diellza had been through it over and over in the last few weeks. They were trying to see the best in forgiveness and understanding that different times and different cultures and upbringing may lead to different mentalities and maybe it was because they were so happy at this point in their life, they decided to give Altin the chance to prove he was a changed man.

He had been in the cafe for well over two months and was never under the impression of being influenced by alcohol, he looked like a man who had made mistakes but looked like he was clearly trying to seek repentance in his final years.

One day in the cafe Steven approached him.

"Where are you staying?" he asked.

"There is a halfway house in Todmorden about 30 minutes from here. I come here on the off chance I can see my dear Diellza, but I can't push because I deserve to be hated," he replied.

"You will come for tea with us tomorrow. If I get the slightest impression that Diellza wants you gone then you are gone," he stated.

"Steven sir. You don't know what this means to me," said Altin.

"Just don't let her down. Everyone deserves a second chance in life. Family is family," Steven softened as he said.

The next evening, Diellza and Steven were feeling on edge about the visit with Altin.

Diellza, though scared, also felt safe with Steven and hoped that if her angels had brought her Steven, then maybe, just maybe, her God and angels would have found a way to forgive her father.

She prepared Byrek, an Albanian vegetable pie. It sent an aroma around the old kitchen with the magical ingredients of feta cheese, spinach, tomatoes and cabbage, she managed to get hold of a bottle of Raki, but this was only as a novelty to offer one with the meal, and in some way a test for her father, she prepared Turkish espresso to deter Altin from being the drunken lout she hoped to erase from her past.

There was a knock on the door that echoed. Though somehow Altin managed to make the tone of the knocking sound almost delicate and calm like he was showing respect even for the door.

Diellza stood behind Steven as she took off her apron and Steven then made way to the door.

"Steven!" he said offering a box of Halva, traditional dense sweets.

"Aba," Diellza called.

"Bija," cried Altin as they met to hug.

Altin sobbed more than Diellza but Steven could see that they were both happy to be together. The safety net that was Steven made Diellza forget the worst in her father and just focus on their reunion.

"Raki? Altin?" offered Steven, with a testing element of suspicion to his tone.

"No Steven my son! My Biri. It is so kind of you to have made such effort, but I have not touched a drop since my darling Diellza made me wake up and face the world I was blinded by for so many years," Altin confirmed.

Diellza smiled as she felt a warm truth in her heart that sung like a sonnet, and she reflected this by smiling over to Steven.

The night was a success and it sincerely felt like there was a fantastic new path that they could all eventually stroll down in harmony.

In time, Altin had really proven that all people can do bad things and change, he would help out at the cafe and found that three or four nights a week he would stay at the house. Though the transformation and progression were impressive, Steven would still never let Altin stay at the house when he was not present.

Diellza knew this, Altin knew this, yet it was never formally mentioned, just subtly acknowledged.

Altin spent Christmas and New Year's with Diellza and Steven and everything seemed to fit.

Steven had the family he never had and Diellza had the family she always wanted.

It seemed as though nothing could have ever gone wrong for any of them.

Chapter 10

It was Valentine's Day and Steven had never conformed to what he believed was a billion-dollar industry dressed in red, but he was still out for the day trying to find a gift for Diellza as he knew these were the moments that made her glow and smile.

It was the first time he had gone out and left Altin with her, though there was no worry from any of them as they had formed a fantastic relationship that had grown over the last eight weeks.

A bouquet of roses, box of heart-shaped chocolates and a large 'me to you' grey teddy bear that Steven felt was overpriced but he knew that the tackier the better for his lady.

Steven had to go further into the valleys to find the teddy and found himself at the far end in the outskirts of Elland.

Elland was about 40 minutes from home and the rain was living up to its West Yorkshire reputation.

Travelling back and heading towards the small village of Sowerby bridge, a box van tilted and tipped in the horrific weather causing a pile up all the way back to Elland where Steven was eagerly sat.

Hours had passed and Steven felt a cramp in his right foot from constantly finding the bite in the clutch as he was starting and stopping every few minutes in what turned out to be a five-hour traffic jam.

Steven was frantic because he knew he was late for his date with Diellza and he had no means of getting hold of her.

As the traffic cleared his car engine revved and growled up fuel. He swerved to the left through a tiny town called 'Friendly' and sped off down through the country lanes to get home.

Pulling into the driveway Steven was anxious because he was late, but he was so excited to see Diellza and to give her, her obligatory seasonal gifts. Running through the door he shouted.

"HAPPY VALENTINES DAY! I'm so so sorry I'm late," he couldn't finish his words as the site he came home to was something no person should have to ever see. Sound changed to muffled noise and his eyes inherited a strobe light effect to his vision with flashes of lines and what looked like scribbles and doodles on a notepad.

Diellza was in the corner of the kitchen. Tucked into the wall with a tiny cloth hiding her modesty. Her legs were dripping in blood and her hair was sticky and overtaking her face, with only a wine-red swollen ball type bruise under her eye.

Diellza could not speak; Steven dropped his pointless gifts and fell to his knees.

"Babai," Diellza kept sobbing. It was Albanian for father.

"DID HE DO THIS?" Steven absolutely raged in a pitch to his voice that he never knew he had.

Diellza just pulled her knees up further and covered her face. She was black and blue and had little sign of character left in her expression. Steven went to hold her and she screamed.

She shouted, "Leave me alone!"

"You leave me alone!"

It pierced through his temple as he felt completely responsible, not only for leaving her with this inevitable fucking monster but for being a catalyst as to how he got back in her life. He felt physically sick.

Steven could not stand, could not sit. He hated himself.

He called Joyce and then called an ambulance. He was empty, angry, cold, furious, bitter, vulnerable and unreasonable.

He watched the Neon Lights take Diellza away and he stomped down the driveway to her car grabbing the half-drunken bottle of Raki that was on the marble top. Realising it had blood-marked fingertips around the nozzle he spat on the lid and took a sip. He got in Diellza's car and drove off failing to even turn the lights on.

Heading to the halfway house in Todmorden he replayed what he imagined having happened.

Altin's dirty fat belly groping Diellza, her screaming and waiting for Steven to come and rescue her, his huge hands thumping into Diellza's sweet innocent face, Altin ripping her pants to her knees and raping his own daughter as he muzzled her mouth with his flabby arms. The fear and the atrocity his poor wife went through from a man she fled and Steven brought him back into her life.

Steven did not check one traffic light. He didn't look in his mirror once. He didn't even put his seatbelt on or wait for the frost to melt on the windscreen. He just drove until he arrived at the house.

Sat only for a few seconds waiting for somebody to come or go so he could gain entry; Steven could not wait any longer.

It was an old four-bedroom conversion property that had become four flats. Steven smashed through the bay windows of the front flat with a wet log that was in the tatty garden.

"Where is Altin?" he demanded.

A frantic young couple cried as they exclaimed that they know nobody by that name. He just walked through their door into the foyer.

He saw Altin walking upstairs in his brown coat.

Altin looked back and panicked.

"It was a mistake," he pleaded as he started to run up the staircase.

Steven grabbed the tail of his coat and pulled him down as his foot gave way and twisted him to his fall. The scream sounded like the squelching scratch of a thousand fingernails scraping down one chalkboard. The irony in the scene as a man so huge making the noise of a pig in a slaughterhouse.

Steven looked into Altin's eyes and announced in a viciously deep and gritty tone, "DEAD MAN!" and Steven beat him senseless.

Lights from the other three flats come on as they came into the landing. Two couples and one old lady all tried to hold Steven back as the blood from Altin's face sprayed over Steven's mouth as he could not be refrained from conflicting endless blows to his cowardly face.

Altin was crying, begging, sobbing, pleading, "Let me go, let me go," and Steven punched and punched until his knuckles were jelly. His teeth crunched as he grinded to channel his anguish.

Steven blanked and fell into Altin but not before head butting and biting until the sound of a muffled police siren hummed into the background.

The police could not control his rage, it took two tasers and still Steven was crying:

"I'm sorry! I'm sorry Diellza," he sobbed.

The police took Altin away into an ambulance and Steven was taken away by the police.

Chapter 11

Sitting in a waiting room under police custody, Steven was nursing a broken wrist in one hand with shattered knuckles in both. He was awaiting results from the Cardiologist as his heart was uncontrollably overactive.

Sat with his head looking at the tired floor, he blanked out the moans and screams from all the drunks that were taking up the emergency room. His right leg was bouncing up and down and he was lost; completely void of comprehension.

He told the police that he would not go anywhere until he knew Diellza was okay and that she was safe.

The police ignored all protocol because they believed in Steven's eyes and in his cry, though not acceptable, the crime Altin committed on his daughter was enough to drive any man into a moment of insanity.

Declining a cup of water, Steven just grinded the bottom deck of his teeth onto his thumbnail as it rubbed his swollen lip. There were scratches all over his eyes where Altin tried to poke through Steven's eyes in defence. Steven was ashamed that even Altin's defence tactics were that of a coward.

Steven felt no pain, he was nursing his wounds to remind him that they were there. The only pain he felt was the pain Diellza went through whilst he was stuck in traffic with a stupid giant bear. When he should have been home to prevent this.

Steven ignored the fact that this was just an inevitable ticking time bomb and held himself completely accountable.

One of the police guards offered him a piece of paper towel to clean his lip. Steven knew it was a polite gesture so as he looked to the officer, he took it, but he did not wipe his face, he just crushed it up and over the hours in the waiting room he just tore pieces off one bit by bit over time.

The room was almost silent, yet all Steven could hear was the echoing seconds finger on the giant clock and the vibrating of the vending machine in its monotone note, sulking amongst all the people waiting in pain. A split second passed, and he emerged from a daydream to hear a muffled, "Steven!"

Then louder, "STEVEN!" called one of the officers.

"Your results are in and we need to get you ready to come with us," hesitated the officer.

"I need to know if Diellza is okay," he pleaded calmly.

The Doctor was with the other officer in the corner, talking quietly. Steven noted the officer's look over his left shoulder with a sympathetic glare towards him. Steven started to feel strength in his knuckles and squeeze as he feared the worse, but the damage done to them from the thrashing he gave Altin woke him up as the physical pain managed to channel through.

He was fearing the worst as the officer and the Doctor walk slowly towards him.

"Diellza," he cried aloud.

"Diellza is fine Steven. There is a lot of trauma but there is no long-term damage physically."

"I would suggest you let us refer her to the Live well psychiatrist. It is a programme that deal with these cases regularly," said the doctor with a sympathetic tone of concern.

"She has nobody other than me. Please make sure she is looked after," said Steven assuming that he would be sent away for what he intended to be the murder of Altin.

The officers informed and assured Steven that she would be protected and supported through her ordeal. You could tell that the officers hated being on duty for this situation because the way in which Diellza was left would haunt the dreams of any person on scene. The fact that her own dad could do this just amplified its horrific content.

"And him?" asked Steven with a sharp slice of frosted resent in the question itself, he wanted to know because he wanted him dead. Steven didn't want to leave Diellza but he knew that the only way he would sleep easy knowing she was safe was that Altin was rid of this earth.

"He made it through," sighed the officer. "He is in custody, and he will never go near your wife again. He is in the country illegally and is wanted at home also for three counts of sexual assault and battery. It's in the hands of the justice system now but it's my understanding that be it here or home, he will not be released in this lifetime."

Steven held his breath, filled his diaphragm and closed his eyes and let out the biggest sigh. With each molecule of oxygen leaving his body was a separate emotion. The trauma of Diellza he has to forever replay, the joy that Altin is never going to get her again, the sorrow that he didn't kill him, the joy that he isn't a murderer, the fear that he would have been okay and capable of murder, the love he knows he feels for Diellza that allows him to be okay with murder, the fear of being locked away, the strangest insignificant fear of who will open the cafe and manage the business, the physical pain that had now started to channel through him, the sadness and terror he inflicted on Altin's neighbours as they witnessed his beating Altin to the ground. He wondered if he hit anybody on the drive down to Todmorden as he had only tunnel vision. The stupid bear. He wondered where the bear was. He couldn't shift the thought of this gigantic daft 'Me to You' bear that he held so accountable for the mess that was about to change his life.

Then he inhales another sharp breath.

"Can I see her before we go?" he asked.

"Certainly Steven," replied the officer and he ushered him through the back rooms of the hospital.

Through the corridors were cries of people in little curtain covered booths, the smell of TCP found his nose and he was holding onto this smell as it held a memory of when he bumped his knee as a child. It was like that was the only other occasion he felt real physical pain and it honed in as a nostalgic memory to him.

Outside the room where Diellza was being cared for, were two other guards. The policemen gave each other the nod and they moved aside and opened the double doors.

Diellza's tired, hungry and lifeless face lit up the second she saw her husband. Steven kissed her and they both felt pain as they kissed but it was worth the pain as their friendship and connection were all they needed.

Steven pleaded to her and cried and apologised and Diellza smiled and kissed his hands as she assured him it was okay.

The Doctor came into the room and asked them for a minute of their time. The police were also cautious of the time and were explaining that they had to take Steven with them soon.

Diellza was distraught in learning that Steven had to go.

"You are the strongest person I have met Diellza. Do not lose that strength or let him take it from you. Otherwise, it was all for nothing," hammered Steven.

"I have some bad news," said the Doctor.

"You lost the baby," she said looking lost into Diellza's broken expression.

Diellza and Steven hadn't even known they were pregnant.

Steven froze. Diellza broke into further pieces. She didn't know she had any pieces left but more shattered right there and then.

Steven felt his inner voice saying, "Say something! Do something! Make her okay!" but he was frozen.

His unreadable reaction also made Diellza feel like he was angry at her for being pregnant, as though he thought she knew and hid it from him. Diellza feared Steven thought she planned to trap him but he didn't think this at all. He just could not take any more information in and simply froze.

She turned away, covered the sheet over her face and demanded everyone to leave.

Even then Steven didn't say anything. He held his hands out so that the police could cuff him.

"We don't have to put these on Steven," said one officer.

"I don't want to be treated any different officer. Just take me away please."

The other officer cuffed Steven as tears streamed down his face.

"Diellza!" said Steven. Looking as he hoped she would turn. He wasn't sure of what to say. He thought about telling her he loved her, but something stopped him.

"Don't let him take your strength or it was all for nothing," he scattered as he held in tears of a cry that was about to combust into a storm.

The police took Steven away into the back of a van and he placed his back, upright, straight adjacent to the van walls and looked up to the roof of the van and long tears rolled down to the floor as if a tap had been unblocked after many years.

Steven knew right then that he had lost Diellza in more ways than one.

Chapter 12

June

It's been two years.

Steven pleaded 'Guilty to Grievous Bodily Harm with intent to kill'. He was advised to plead momentary insanity, but he declined this advice and declined representation. He explained to the judge that whilst he was not sorry for the pain he inflicted on Altin, it was an attack on filth and scum and that he posed no threat to any other person in a civilised society.

He served only two years of this sentence due to having no previous convictions and due to the nature of the motive along with exceptional behaviour whilst incarcerated. He was offered early release.

During his time in HMRC Manchester institution, he kept to himself socially. He buried his head into development projects for the rehabilitation of addicts which granted him enough of the guards' respect to be recommended to go back into society.

It was only a month after the attack that he was sentenced. It was clear that the judge did not want to deliver the outcome provided to Steven but the attack was so brutal that it could not go unpunished.

He asked Diellza not to visit him as he didn't want her to travel to Manchester week in week out. He asked her to promise she would remain strong and continue her studies. He requested this and yet felt somewhat deflated by the fact that she adhered to his request.

For two years he had only communicated through letters. Though week in week out they would send them, the content shrunk and they become obligatory notes with very little information.

The last letter Steven sent to Diellza was a very hard letter to write. It was brief and simple. It read;

Dear Diellza

It's clear to me that the events that took place on that awful day have impacted us in a significant way.

It has led us into a darkness where light can never be permitted. We got so close to having something we never knew we wanted. But I can't shake the feeling that I am to blame for inviting misery into our home. A misery that you once went through great lengths to avoid. For this, I am so so sorry.

I know I asked you not to visit. I asked you to be strong. I hope you are. I know you are in fact because you are the strongest person I know.

I am giving you an out.

I will grant you a divorce. You will most certainly stay in the house. It holds nothing for me, and you always stayed true to our arrangement.

I thank you for knowing me.

All my heart and forever thinking fondly of you.

Steven x

Diellza never replied.

As the iron gates swung open, Steven shook the guard's hand and walked to the taxi that was waiting for him.

He could have called his non-biological father, but it only occurred to him when getting his release notice that his dad didn't even know that he had been sent to prison, so he swiftly overruled that option.

He considered asking one of the ladies from the cafe, but he didn't want to damage any shred of respect they may have had for him by asking them to collect, what he considered himself, a jail thug, from prison, not to mention it was 40 minutes away from West Yorkshire.

The officials arranged his taxi for him.

"Where to?" the driver asked.

Steven didn't want to say 'Home' as he was unsure if Diellza would want to see him. He had not told her that he was getting released. It had only been a month since his letter, but her lack of reply made him feel like she was happy to accept the divorce. He never received any paperwork but there was none to be expected in only a month. He was nervous. But he had no other place he could go so he gave the driver his home address.

Driving through the village, he lowered his shoulders as he passed the cafe. It was still busy but he didn't want anybody to see him. Pulling up the lane he saw a woman pushing a grey Victorian Pram with huge silver wheels with shiny spokes. There was a white umbrella offering shade to the baby. He instantly thought about how things would have been if they had the baby they never knew they were having. He felt robbed even though there was no plan. He imagined what their boy or girl would have looked like now, had everything been different. He got to the beginning of the lane that leads to the driveway and told the driver he would walk from there.

As his first step took a crunch onto the orange stones that sounded like a packet of crisps being squashed, he felt the ghost of his former self-driving through his body at full speed in Diellza's Volvo that Valentine's evening.

He turned his head as though he was watching the invisible car swoosh past. He turned back and headed to the house.

The once alive, beautiful proud building had gone. The hanging flower baskets were dead, the grass was growing through the cracks on the dirty flags. The water fountain was green with moss and slime. The lights were off and curtains all open and the windows were dirty.

In Steven's eyes, she had gone home. Maybe to her uncle's cottage in Poland.

Diellza would not have left the house like this. He felt so sad that she had gone but he felt that bit more comfortable about putting the key in the door and turning it knowing that she would not be there on the other side to look at him with the hate he believed she carried for him.

He rattled the keychain and pushed the key slightly up as he turned it right and pushed the door open brushing past several months-worth of post built up on the door mat. This confirmed his assumption.

"She's gone," he whispered to himself.

Steven walked into the Library and Diellza was sitting in his green armchair. His heart broke as he saw her sat still from behind. There was an empty glass in her hand hanging off her thumb and finger and a spill patch on the floor. The bottle of Gin on the table was empty.

Steven ran over to check if she was okay. Her white nightdress was creased, she still looked beautiful but drawn out.

"Diellza!" he shakes.

Her eyes opened with a sprinkle of blinks as she saw him. She was still, lay with her head tilted slightly but her eyes focused to a wide-open glair.

"Steven? Am I dreaming or am I in heaven?" she whispered.

"I'm home, Diellza," he smiled. "I thought you were dead," he gasped with relief.

Diellza stands up as she released the empty glass. She rolled the tips of her fingers through his face as though she was checking the sculpting of a model that could only be a recreation of him. She was mapping out his cheeks, his mouth. She drew a line over the scratch on his eye that was inflicted by the monster she once called her father and she let go of her weight and landed into his arms.

"I am dreaming," she said as she kissed him and gripped him with every single muscle and limb she could actively control.

Over the next few months, they were very nervous around each other. They would go on many walks and spend all their time together. They would hold hands and hug but there would still be very little intimacy beyond that. Steven felt unsure if he should or could go near her after what she had suffered and Diellza feared he may not have wanted to.

They held each other most nights but would talk very little about the last two years. They never mentioned their unborn child, but both wanted to so badly.

They were both so damaged by the events that all they knew they could give to each other and all they needed from each other was to be in the same company.

By fractions of deciphered conversations and slight offerings of information they both discovered new things about each other.

Steven was writing all about his family, the very little pieces he had known and was looking to learn all about his ancestry whilst in jail.

On one occasion, Anne decided to visit Steven whilst he was in jail. She never told Joyce or Barbara that she was going and both Steven and Anne never mentioned it afterwards, but she wanted to tell Steven about his birth parents. Anne new his mother slightly growing up and would also speak with Brian over the years after she passed until Brian moved closer to Manchester.

Steven discovered that his birth father was called Esteban. The circumstance behind him and Steven's mother separating was not one with any malice on their parts.

His mother was called Tina and she met Esteban in Majorca.

Brian, his wife and Tina had a family villa out there and would go several times a year. Esteban lived on the same hill with his family. It was not a holiday fling; they were childhood friends. As they came of age, they developed a romance.

Brian and his wife were aware of it and were perfectly fine with it, they merely observed with caution, but young love must be left to blossom and so that's what they did.

Eventually, Tina and Esteban explored further, and in that summer, they tried to tell his parents that they were in love.

As they were both so young and came from different cultures and religious faith, his parents forbid their relationship. They were of legal consenting age, but they were raised with old fashioned morals by old fashioned people.

When Esteban's parents realised that they would still communicate, they insisted that Tina be cut out of their son's life.

When Brian, his wife and Tina returned home, they learned of her pregnancy. Brian contacted Estaban's father to tell him, but they refused to acknowledge this and almost immediately moved away from the hill before Tina was able to make contact herself.

Brian tried over the years to find Estaban, as he did when searching for Steven, but unfortunately, there was no trace at all.

After learning this, Steven became obsessed with the meaning of names as he learnt that Diellza comes from the meaning 'sun'. It conjures up the image of the royal women of Albania. You have to pronounce the name as 'Di-Yeh-Zah'. An inmate told him this and so he started learning what all other names mean.

Diellza had become so depressed by all of the events but most of all, the absence of Steven.

She learnt that her dad got extradited back to Albania and he tried to write several times, but she burnt every single letter.

She thought about tracking her own mother down, but she couldn't. She didn't want her mumma to have to address her own shame of being raped or being pimped out like a whore to Altin's seedy friends and even worse, she dreaded the idea of investigating her whereabouts on the fearful presumption that she may have already taken her own life. She just had to emotionally disconnect.

The depression got so strong that she considered taking her own life but her promise to Steven was to stay strong and she kept it.

She quit teaching. She took it upon herself to manage the cafe and the three ladies took so well to her, teaching her everything they knew. She applied everything she had into the cafe and evolved it into an external catering business offering fine cuisines to weddings and conferences. She had to do anything to avoid the house. She would only come home to sleep. She would only use the backdoor as she was scared of the front door as it reminded her of that awful night.

She could not let the house go because it was Steven's only link to his past but the idea of sleeping in the house where she was viciously raped taunted her always. Until she saw it as a way of therapy to face her demons and forced herself to live with it.

One Sunday they were making lunch and Diellza slipped on the floor. Right by the spot where Steven found her. She noticed marks on the skirting board where she was struggling, and she melted. She started wailing.

Steven came running and could make no sense of her until he too saw the marks. Steven stood and left the room.

Diellza was distraught and didn't know where he had gone. *Why has he left me?* she thought. Moments later he returned with four tins of paint stacked on one another. He opened the top draw of the kitchen drawers and pulled out a butter knife.

He opened the lids of all the tubs and took Diellza's hand and said to her with a 'slightly psychotic yet excited' glare in his eye, "Come on! Grab one," and handed her a tub of paint.

With confusion in her gaze, she got up and sniffed out the last few breaks of snot and tears and took hold of a tin of pink paint.

"Now throw it!" dared Steven.

SPLAT!!!

The paint in its mouldy splash of an unmixed texture landed on the corner of the wall against the beautiful wood, climbing down to the degrading marks on the wall!

"Another!" he offered.

She took the blue tin of paint and the same again.

SPLAT!!!

This time she shouted: "GO TO HELL."

"Another!" he continued.

SPLAT!!!

Again, but louder she yelled: "GO TO HELL."

"ANOTHER!!!" screamed Steven, and once more she covered the walls in a clementine orange paint, yelling:

"Go to hell! You can't beat me!"

The cry turned into a sob then turned into a laugh. Steven and Diellza found anything they could that would open and would stick. Steven threw a bag of flower in the air. Diellza emptied three bottles of wine and threw them in the air, spinning with the lid off and all over her and Steven. They threw eggs, milk, empty cereal boxes and were laughing their hearts out. It was their way of de-cleansing the house and in turn themselves. They were in complete bliss as all the rules left their system and they gained some sort of power and control over their life. They found a place to rest their grief. It was within each other.

Covered in paint, and paste constructed by sugar and washing up liquid, they laughed as they slipped to the ground and playfully covered each other in jam and sauces and blackcurrant juice. Their liberation took them back to each other and they chased each other down the halls until they reached the bathroom and shared a shower.

This was the moment that they found their intimacy again and they found themselves completely naked, kissing each other passionately as their hands held each other's faces. They were both petrified and nervous about being in this moment again, but their chests gravitated so strong it was like they were magnetically stuck on each other.

The following morning, Diellza woke up to find that Steven was not there. She went downstairs wearing only his shirt and saw the chaos that they created.

Through the conservatory, she noticed Steven outside so she made her way to the door. On the patio, he had set up fresh juice and breakfast for her. Continental meats, a fresh box of cereal, blueberries and strawberries with a pot of tea. There was an old milk bottle with freshly picked lavender and a newspaper for her. Looking over to him with a smile that cannot be faked, she was about to speak as he interrupted.

"We will start from the beginning. Build from the outside and create our own memories," he smiled as he was digging the dead flowers out of the hanging baskets that he had taken down.

He walked over and kissed her head and said, "Welcome home, my wife."

Through the August, September and October, they completely transformed the house. They woke her up, decorated all the rooms and had so much fun in the process. They found that they were talking about everything and anything, they were flirting, playing together, reading to each other, cheating at boardgames together and in general learning so many more things about each other and it was wonderful.

One particular morning, Diellza walked into the kitchen and stood by the deep ceramic Belfast sink. She saw Steven on the driveway. She swirled out her coffee cup and elevated slightly off the base of her foot onto her toes to lean over enough to see who he was talking to.

She peered over and noticed that Steven was talking to Stephanie.

Diellza's heart dropped as she saw Steven give Stephanie the most affectionate hug. Stephanie was smiling and they looked, through Diellza's interpretation, like they were supposed to be with one another. She saw a look within Steven that she only ever recognised when he was with Stephanie or talking about Stephanie. Steven hugged her as she sat in her car, and as he turned, Diellza promptly ducked down and ran into the other room.

Walking into the house, Steven looked flush and shouted, "Diellza." He came into the front room and asked her, "Shall we eat out tonight?"

"Sure. That would be nice," she replied hoping he would bring up the fact that the love of his life had just stopped by. But he didn't.

"Perfect," he said. "I'll make a reservation then," and smiled as he walked off into the kitchen.

Diellza sat with a computing look on her face trying to not let her thoughts lead her to a sad or negative place whilst struggling to understand any scenario other than Stephanie telling Steven that she is ready for him and that Steven may consider leaving her for Stephanie.

All she could do was sit and hope she was wrong; and wait to be proven otherwise, as confronting Steven would only make her appear to be an insecure wife. Afterall, in what she sometimes believed Steven saw her in his eyes, she was at heart, only an arrangement.

Chapter 13

It had only been a few weeks since Stephanie stopped by but Diellza had not been able to shift her unsure feelings of worry.

She had not let Steven see this and he had been no different to her.

She had been going to bed a lot earlier, her skin had come out with sores and spots on her face but she held the fact that they were going into winter accountable, along with the stress she had been carrying on her mind wondering into a world where Steven and Stephanie were destined to be together.

One morning, Diellza was at the cafe, and she spoken on the telephone with Steven, who was at home going through the accounts for their, now two businesses.

She suggested having a romantic meal as she had something she wanted to talk to him about. She was deciding if she should confront the fact that she saw them on the driveway, but she was unsure. If it was perfectly innocent then she would look crazy, Steven could wonder why she kept it quiet for several weeks. They would both feel an abolishment of trust as Steven never brought it up and Diellza was peeking over at them without ever saying anything.

Steven held the phone with one hand and was in a perfectly happy mood. He told Diellza he could not wait to have a romantic meal. He told her that everything they needed was already in the fridge and that she should set off home at

5 p.m, then he would have it all on the table set for her with a steaming hot bath running for her afterwards.

Steven went into the bathroom to check if he had plenty of bath salts and candles as he wanted his wife to completely soothe and relax. He looked in the cupboard and saw a pregnancy test. Clear Blue. Easy to read. Results in two minutes. He looked at the box that instructed 'a plus sign is pregnant and a minus is not pregnant'. He pulled the test from within the box and staring right at him was a 'clear blue plus'.

"Pregnant?" he muttered.

Steven put it down and headed downstairs. he left the radio and lights on and took his jacket and his keys and left the house.

Six o'clock arrived and Diellza opened the door.

"Honey, I'm home," in a silly American accent she called.

"Steven?" she called again.

Slightly confused she looked around the house. There was no food made, the lights were on and the radio was on. Steven said that he would have tea made. She began to panic and tried to call his mobile phone. It went straight to voicemail.

Diellza went upstairs to the bathroom and spotted the test.

"Oh my God," she worried.

She only found out herself a few days before but wanted to do another one after a couple of days to be sure, before she told Steven. She was unsure of complications that may have arisen and wanted advice. She wanted to test the water and see if it was something Steven was happy with and now he had gone. She thought he was clearly upset by the news of a baby on the way.

Two hours had passed by and she was sitting by the island in the kitchen waiting for him to come home so that she could apologise for not telling him and assure him she wanted his full and honest opinion on everything. All of a sudden, the idea of talking about Stephanie was so far out of the window that it was not even a minor thought.

She could hear an engine of a car coming down the crunchy driveway and through the dark chilled air she saw the beams of the headlights and ran to the door waiting to see her husband.

Swinging the door open she shouted to him, "Steven."

However, it was not Steven. It was the police.

She knew before they got to the door that something was wrong and as they delivered the harrowing news that he had been involved in a collision, she took her coat and rushed to the back of the police car.

Chapter 14

It had been two weeks and Steven was still bed-bound in the hospital assisted by machinery.

Diellza had been by his side day in day out. She bathed him and read to him and sang to him. She was fearful she would lose him but at no point would she give up hope that her beloved Steven, her charming husband; the man that allowed her to become the strong happy woman she had become; the man that was able to demonstrate so much courage in growing himself as a person and allowing himself to love the way he did, is going anywhere.

His ocean blue eyes were closed and she felt it was unfair to the world that nobody may see them ever again.

She would talk to him about their wedding day. Reciting the memories and realising that they were not at all a farce but in fact a magical couple and linked it all back to that magical day. Stuffing their faces with chicken and mushroom *Vol-au-vents* and dancing to Abba in a room full of strangers. She pointed out that there were sparks flying around that day and whilst they were at the time mistook for two broken people fixing a loophole in each other's universe, the complete truth was that the universe wanted them to spark, light and shine through their days.

Diellza thanked Steven's sleeping heart for the tiny simple things, like how her nervous blinking had disappeared and all the other silly things that mount to great accomplishments when realising the love of your life has helped you learn things about yourself or forget things you never knew you disliked about yourself until they had already faded away.

The doctors knew that there was no point in asking her to ever leave as she simply would not, so they let her be.

One Saturday afternoon she was reading him a story that her uncle used to tell her. It was in Albanian but she just wanted to share this perfect memory with him. As her eyes were buried in the book, she heard his delicately dehydrated voice, "Please don't stop reading, my Diellza."

Diellza thought it was in her mind and so she continued with a smile as though she has imagined him at home.

Her memory trailed in her head to a daydream where they were at home. He was in the bath covered in suds and she was sat on the floor next to him reading to him. He mocked her Albanian accent, and she cupped her hand full of bubbles from the bath in her palm and blew it in his face and so he then dragged her in the bath. She was soaked and then she snapped out to see that his eyes were open.

"Wakey wakey, sweetheart," she lightly announces. She is strangely calm and doesn't want to startle him in case its either a dream; or if it's reality, then she doesn't want to scare him back into his coma.

"Kiss me, Diellza," he says.

They are both unsure as to why, but he was wide awake. They spent the whole evening talking and playing cards. None of them mentioned the baby. Through no reason other than they are just one in this moment.

They talked until three o'clock in the morning until Steven begged her to go home and refresh and rest.

"I'll be here in the morning," he promised. So, she kissed his head and left the hospital room.

Walking down the well-lit hospital corridors, she glided the tips of her fingers down the grey plastic bumpers on the walls. She felt as though she was flying home. Happy that Steven was back and with her. She could not wait to begin the rest of her life with him.

As she left Steven shouted the Doctor. Diellza was unsure of the meaning of this conversation but something inside her wanted to just ignore her instincts. With all that had happened she decided to abandon her intrigue at that point and focus on brighter days ahead and merely assume that Steven was asking for an update on his progress.

Chapter 15

The next day, Diellza woke and dressed quickly. She reached for a milk bottle and swirled it out to fill it with fresh lavender.

Almost skipping to the hospital ward, she entered to see Steven. She opened the door to find that he was not there.

Innocently she assumed he was having a test done or being placed in a recovery ward as the night before he was a picture of health.

"Where have you moved my husband to?" she kindly asked.

"Oh, my darling! You don't know; bless your soul," replied the downhearted looking lady by the desk.

"Let me call the doctor immediately," she said.

Diellza knew what she was about to hear. She denied it but she knew.

The Doctor explained to her how he went quietly in his sleep…there was a complication in his heart, he explained that this was not the same as his mum had suffered and that it was the crash that had caused clotting around his heart.

The strangest thing is that although she felt her world had broken and crashed, she didn't break or cry. She just froze and for a split second replayed every single memory she had of him.

The laughs, hurt, cries, shy moments, getting to know him, loving him, losing him, getting him back. It flooded through like a stormy river bursting through a man-made dam and as it reached the point of impact, she heard an echo of his voice in her head tell her, *Stay strong, my darling Diellza.*

The doctors left her alone and gave her an envelope addressed 'to the love of my entire life'.

For weeks, she held onto it but then she finally did what she expected he wanted and met with the girl he loved and Diellza told her, "Here's your letter," she said to Stephanie.

Diellza didn't break in the way her former self may have once broken. In fact, she just toughened up, walked away and carried on.

It was months after Steven had died and she was heavily pregnant doing the accounts in the cafe. It was closed yet she heard the doorbell go. 'Baaa Dooop' Diellza was never going to replace this horrible doorbell as it became a symbol of Steven for the three ladies. 'Baaa Dooop'.

She was the only one left and the sign said 'closed' but she turned to find Stephanie standing there.

Standing nervously, clearly upset but paying her utmost respect to Diellza, she stared and grimaced.

"I came for him, you know? One day on your driveway, I told him I loved him too. I begged him to leave you and come with me," she said with a twitch in her eye and the envelope in her hand.

"Goodbye, Diellza," said Stephanie as she handed the brown envelope back to Diellza and walked away.

Chapter 16

My darling Diellza

Thank you for teaching me how to love, for watching over me throughout the best years of my life and for understanding me as only soulmates could!

I am not scared of where I am going because I know I will see you and our child again one day.

I left home that day to arrange something for you. Your uncle's old house in Poland. It's yours. I bought it for you. Now our baby can share your happiest memory with you and visit your favourite place whenever you like.

You have become the strongest woman I know and my best friend. Our child is going to be so happy, so loved and so wonderful.

I promise you I will be with you every single day.
You are the one true love of my entire life.
I love you, Diellza. Forever and always.

Steven

Diellza pulls the letter away from her face as it is the 100th time she has read the letter to her son over the last five years. This time from the top of the breezy hillside of her late uncle's land as she snuggles their son into her arms.

"This Stevie is the gift your father gave to us before he went to heaven," she grinned.

"What was he like, Mummy?" asked the little boy blinking like a younger Diellza.

"He was a lot like you, my darling. I will race you to the bottom. Come on," she joked as she ran off into the picturesque backdrop.

Running through the tall uncut grass, she sees her baby boy so full of life and she envisages Steven running alongside them until they are at the cottage gate.

"Do you miss him, Mummy?" pants the little boy as they stop to catch a breath.

"Every single day, my boy. But, you see, love is so perfect and wonderful that if you get to truly feel it! And even if the loss seems unbearable, son. If you have truly felt it, hold it and never let it go, then it's eternal."

"I love you, Mummy," says little Steven.

With the biggest grin on her face, she looks to the pale blue sky and breathes in the spring air breeze as she holds him so tight and replies, "We love you too, Steven."

As baby Steven playfully cheats and sets off running a new race ahead of Diellza and runs off, Diellza catches a moment alone and whispers to the air, "I love you, my darling husband. Forever and always."